<u>Dedication</u>

I will like to dedicate this book to my twin sister, Chonte' Bridges. Like me, you have endured so much pain and tragedy. There were many times you thought suicide was the answer, but God stepped in each time. No matter how long it took, you were determined to make a change. Through all you have experienced, you didn't stay there. But you got back up each time and kept pushing forward. Your dedication became my motivation. You are a prime example of Transforming Victim to Victorious.

I also dedicate this book to my son, Tyler Williams. Though you are young now, this story is true experiences that I, your mom, have endured. There were many times I wanted to end it all and just give up. However, it was finding out that I was pregnant with you that gave me so much life. You are my miracle child, because when the enemy said death, God said life. As you grow older, you will learn more about the obstacles I, your mom, has overcome. Use this as motivation to overcome every storm that will come your way.

Never give up; you are a King's kid.

You're Victorious!

Acknowledgements

First and foremost, I want to that God. Many people are unable to speak of what they have gone through, and many have not survived. However, I am so grateful that God saw fit to use me as a vessel, to bring others to his kingdom. We easily forget why we go through these situations, and become blinded by the pain because it hurts so much. We have to remember everything we go through is so that God gets the glory. It is to show how God is true to his word, and how he will bring us out. Our testimonies are used to be an example to others of Gods goodness. I am just so glad he used me.

Secondly I have to acknowledge the one who has held my hand every step of the way, the love of my life, Ronald Williams. When I wanted to give up, when I wanted to cry, when I was indecisive, and much, much more, he supported my every decision. At the same time, he pushed me to achieve all that I can. He is the indispensable link, to my chain of success, and without him, I am not complete.

In addition, I have to thank my aunt, my first best friend, the one I can tell all and not be judged, Randa Shanta Scott. Girl, I love you so much, as well as my cousins, Shantaza, Javis, and

Khadijah. Without you all, I would have lost my sanity many years ago. Because of you, I am the woman I am today. Everything I know about being a woman, I learned from you. I can trust you with my life and know all will be well. There is nothing I wouldn't do for you. You were an open ear in this process, and you understand all that I have experienced and never thrown it back at me, neither did you diminish my experiences. You took it for what it was, embraced my pain and pushed me to grow. I love you!

To my mother Traci Scott, our relationship has grown, and because of God and God alone, I was able to first forgive and secondly love. The bible says "Honor your mother and father for thy days shall be longer".

To my grandparents, Mr. and Mrs. Scott, I love you all for everything you have done for me. My appreciation and love cannot be explained by words. Thank you for teaching me who God is. It's because of that foundation, I am alive today. The bible says, "Raise a child up in the way that they shall go and they will never depart". No matter the pain, the struggle, the obstacle, the issue, it all led me back to Christ and I am so thankful.

Finally, to my mentor, publisher, best-selling author, and CEO of Just Wright Publications, Author Sean Wright, I'm new to the game and you're true to the game. You have taught me everything I know about the industry. You have taken me out of my comfort zone and challenged me to be and do so much more. You have opened so many doors for me and without your expertise and honesty; I would have drowned in the process. Thank you for your continuing education in this field and being the best publisher the world can offer. You're the Greatest, and I am excited where our teamwork can lead us in the future.

In Memory of:

**James Alexander Bridges: 1941-2011**

Daddy, oh how proud you will be. I have grown up to be what you thought I would be and more. You use to call me "motor mouth", and now it will be used to reach those who have been victimized. I remember how much it broke you down when I first told you I was molested. No one else has ever responded so sincerely. Thinking about still breaks my heart of how much it hurt you. You always taught me to be strong and I always admired your strength alone in having to endure that pain of your daughter being hurt. You are gone but far from forgotten and I know you are smiling down on me.

Victim to Victorious

HEY GOD, DID YOU GET MY MESSAGE?

CHAPTER 1

I'll never forget, it was a Wednesday and we had just left church yet again. My grandparents were true followers of Christ, and we went to church every day, sometime multiple times on Sundays. This is the life I had come to know living with them. I used to complain about it, but quickly realized that anything was better than living with my mother who was strung out on drugs. Luckily my grandparents had come to our rescue before The Bureau of Child Welfare could get their hands on me, my twin sister Dana, and my two brothers Cory, and Jason. Yes I was a twin and we were fraternal; I was night, she was day. She was short and thick, I was tall and slim. I was Jesus and she was Lucifer. That's how most could tell us apart. Then there was my older brother Cory was the closest to me and Dana in age, he only had us by 2 years, where Jason had us by 7. With the exception of Dana and I we all had different dead beat fathers. Jason was actually conceived during a rape that my mom encountered.

I have to admit that although living with my grandparents started out cool, as I got older things got a little rough. When she removed us from our moms home Dana and I were no older than 3years old; much too young to see or understand the strict rules and ways of a religious household. Besides the overbearing influx of religion, there were certain T.V. shows we couldn't watch, certain friends we couldn't have, and many times we were forced to stay in one room and play with each other and out of the way of "grown folks". Even that was eventually adaptable, until one day when I was around 7 or 8 and life as I knew it would become an all-out living hell.

"Dana, Lana. Ya'll stop running through this house. Ya'll see me tryna do my housework. Jason come get your sisters out of my way while I clean up." My grandmother yelled as my sister and I played hide and seek throughout the house.

Within seconds my oldest brother Jason was in the living room adhering to my grandmother's wishes.

"Okay ya'll heard granny. Let's go." Jason said.

"But Jason we're playing hide and seek." I pleaded with puppy dog eyes.

"And ya'll can still play Lana, just not in here." He said.

"Will you play with us?" Dana asked.

"If it will keep you out of granny's hair then yes."

"Yaaay. Okay I'll count and you guys go hide." I said as I covered my eyes and started my countdown.

"1,2,3…."

When I got to ten I uncovered my eyes and began my search for Jason and Dana.

"Ready or not here I come." I said as I searched each level of the house while steering clear of granny.

After coming up empty on the first and second floor I head for the basement. I crept down the steps as to not alert them to my presence. When I reached the bottom of the steps I tip toed around looking in closets and behind large objects. They must have been in the guest bedroom here in the basement; they were making it too easy. As I slowly made my way towards the room, my suspicions were confirmed as I heard them both whispering. They really sucked at this game, or so I thought. You can imagine the look on my face when I opened the door and saw my 15-year-old brother with his pants down and my 7-year-old twin who also had her pants down sitting on his lap. Dana looked scared and confused, while Jason looked like everything, but my big brother.

"Come in, close the door, and take your clothes off." Jason instructed with a look in his eyes I had never seen before. I was always told to obey my older brother so I did as I was told.

I had never felt so much pain in my short lived life. The spot between my legs felt like someone had dumped a garbage can full of fire on it. My sister and I both took turns screaming to the top of our lungs, but we were no match for Granny blasting Mahalia Jackson's greatest hits on her century old record player. Dana and I each took turns kicking, screaming, and biting Jason's hand as he attempted to cover our mouths, but even the two of us were no match for him. Even though the combined violation took all of 22 minutes according to the eerily scary antique cuckoo clock that hung from the wall (that thing always scared the bejeezus out of me.) it seemed like Jason ravished us, wronged us, and robbed us of our pureness and innocence for hours until he let out a huge grunt and rolled over. He warned us both to keep quiet about our "game".

After the tormenting ordeal Dana and I both headed upstairs to our room to sleep off the anguish or at least attempt to. We both walked slowly and gingerly up the steps, and right passed Granny with tears streaming down our faces. She looked at us, shook her head, and continued dusting and singing.

CHAPTER 2

I know this is gonna sound crazy but believe it or not the "game" with Jason didn't stop there. Over the next few years he would visit me at night. He would visit Dana as well but not as much; I'm sure it's because I was coming into womanhood much faster than she was. I mean I was only 12 by this time but most people figured me to be in my mid-teens already because of how tall I was. Coming from the streets of Newark most of these fast ass little girls would love the attention I was getting from the older guys. Maybe I would have gotten wrapped up into that too but the things Jason did to me made me hate any and all attention. To this day, I sometimes hold my head down, not knowing how to react to a compliment, thinking everybody wants something. I couldn't even gear up the guts to tell my grandparents because I believe it will do no good at all. They were so worried about how "the church" would look at us that I could never let that secret get out, so it left me to handle the torment all alone.

One night my God Brother Gary was spending the night. He, Jason, and Cory played Nintendo all night until he and Cory tapped out and decided to go to bed. I loved when Gary came and spent time at the house. Gary was really like my big brother. He became my hero when Jason started using me as his personal sex toy years ago. So many times I wanted to tell him what was going on, but granny and Jason had sworn me to secrecy years ago. There were many reasons I loved him around but none more than the fact that I felt safe because Jason would never try and have me with Gary around. Truth be told Jason was scared of Gary the way Cory was scared of Jason; which is why he never came to my defense.

I was asleep in my bed dreaming of a much better place and a much better life when I felt my nightgown slowly being raised. Tears immediately welled up in my eyes as my worst fears were confirmed.

"It's been a while since I had some of this. Come on turn over, you know what's up." Jason whispered.

I attempted to play sleep like I did many times before, but like many times before it did me no good as I was forced over on my back, panties pushed to the side and forcibly penetrated. Jason used to cover my mouth to muffle my screams, but these last few encounters he didn't need to. I had learned that the screams and cries fell on deaf ears throughout the house and the more I fought the longer it took. So I had learned to just lay there and take it. *Jason would eventually get his off, get up and leave then sit down and have "FAMILY" breakfast the next morning as if nothing ever happened. Nigga always had the nerve to ask me to pass him the syrup. Each time he did that I wanted to take a table knife to everyone in the house. I often figured if I killed everyone then they could die with this funky ass secret they kept holding in, and while they were dead I could finally live. But the fact remains that no matter how dysfunctional my family was, they were all I had.*

As I lay there hoping and praying he would hurry up and finish. My prayers were answered in the weirdest way; but answered none the less.

"Yo what the hell are you doing?" was all I heard while it seemed like Jason was magically lifted off of me and thrown through the air.

Before I knew what was going on Gary was on top of Jason beating the pure dee crap out of him. I mean it was like WWE RAW. I sat up in my bed wishing for two things; a bag of popcorn to watch the show, and death to the pervert who had tormented me for so long. Unfortunately I would get neither.

"Gary what are you doing? Get up off of that boy." Granny yelled as she tried to pull him off of Jason.

She was no match for the High School football star so she called for reinforcements. I still lay there enjoying the show as my grandfather, Cory and, Dana came running into my room. It took all of them to pull Gary off of Jason who was now deservingly bloodied, bruised, and unconscious.

"Gary we welcome you into our home and this is what you do?"   Granny said with steam coming from her ears.

"This coward ass dirt bag was raping Lana."

"Oh Gary, that's just a little game that Jason play with the girls. He would never do anything to hurt his sisters. It's just a game; right Dana?" Granny asked Dana as everyone directed their attention her way.

I looked over and Cory was giving her the death stare, as if his eyes was saying *"you bet not say a word."* While I looked over at her with tears in my eyes I mumbled *"Please twin this is the time to save ourselves."* I was begging for her to tell the truth. But I can tell she was too scared to speak up, at least not for me.

"No. Jason aint never did nothing to me and I'm sure he aint never did nothing to Lana either; she always over reacting."

I couldn't believe what I was hearing and immediately surmised that Dana was terrified and rather continue you that turmoil caused by Jason, rather than confess.

"See Gary you done beat that boy senseless and for what? Granny snapped.

"Nah I aint tripping I know what I seen him doing." Gary snapped back confident in his vision.

"How can you be so sure as dark as it was in here?" Granny asked.

I knew exactly how to put an end to all of the bullshit. I nonchalantly walked through the crowd of commotion and into the bathroom, opened the medicine cabinet, and took anything with a prescription written on it to the head. Since no one would save me from my misery…I would save myself.

CHAPTER 3

I woke up and everything around me was white. Unfortunately I was only in the hospital and not in heaven. It took a minute for me to realize that my hands and feet were strapped down to the bed. As my vision began to sharpen I noticed a sign wired to my bed that said "Suicide Watch. " Then I heard someone snoring and looked to my left to see Gary asleep in the chair. I scanned the room and saw nobody else, but that didn't surprise me. While I was comforted and felt extremely good seeing my cousin Gary by my side, I still wished that whoever found me would have just let me die and I immediately started screaming those thoughts.

"Why? Why didn't you just let me die?"

My screams made Gary jump up out of his sleep and the nurse's rush into the room.

"Hey, hey it's okay. I'm right here." Gary said holding my hand as the nurse shot me in the arm with a sedative.

Within seconds I was once again fast asleep.

****
****

Over the next few days they kept me in the hospital in the psych ward on suicide watch. No family ever came to check on me to check on me, but Gary never left my side.

"Uno!" I yelled slamming my card on the table.

"Yo I swear yo ass be cheating." Gary said admitting defeat.

"I aint gotta cheat you to beat you nigga." I stated adamantly.

"Yeah whatever." He joked.

Our game was interrupted by the doctor coming in.

"Good news. After careful consideration, and evaluation you are free to go home today provided you follow up with the therapist I have referred you to, because as much as we love having you around we don't wanna see you back under these conditions. By the way, there's a card under your pillow. "He said giving me the good news while blowing up my spot at the same time.

"See. I knew ya black behind was cheating. Now get ya stuff together so I can take you home."

While that statement should have filled me with joy, it did just the opposite as a tear ran down my face.

"Hey. What you crying for? You going home." Gary asked perplexed.

"That's just it. I don't ever wanna go back there again."

"Oh trust and believe I wasn't takin you back there. You coming to stay with me. Big cuz gonna look out for you from now on."

That was like music to my ears.

"Thanks cuzzo. I really appreciate that. I promise I won't be no trouble."

"Don't sweat it. It's all good let's just get the hell outta here."

"Say no more. Let's be out." I said getting myself together as fast as I could go.

CHAPTER 4

Living with Gary was the coolest shit ever. I mean not only was he my big cousin, but also my best and only friend in the world. Gary was the perfect roommate. He cooked, cleaned, kept the house smelling good, and took pride in the crib. He was also about getting to a dollar. He was one of the most prominent hustlers in the hood. He was liked, well respected, and even feared by some.

Gary allowed me to stay with him on a few small conditions; I had to get straight A's in school, I stay away from boys and I stay away from drugs. And I did exactly as I was told until …

I was sitting home one day doing homework while Gary was out handling business when the phone rang.

"Hello?" I said agitated because the phone ringing had broken my concentration.

"Lana it's me Gary. Listen closely; I want you to grab whatever you can and get the fuck outta the house as fast as you can. Meet me at the park on South Orange Avenue." Gary screamed frantically.

"Wait a minute. Slow down Gary. What the fuck is going on?"

"Look we aint got a lotta time, but long story short the damn cab driver took off with the stash when I jumped out to get a loosie."

I couldn't believe what I was hearing; that had been Gary's personal cab driver for years.

"Okay so what's the big deal? When you see that clown in the hood, you beat him down and make him pay."

"It aint that easy. That package was already paid for and Black and them on their way to the house to pick it up. "

"Okay so what's the problem? Just get ya ass back here and whip up another batch."

"Nah I'll never make it back in time and these aint the niggas you keep waiting so get the hell out of the house and meet me before they bust in there and hurt you in order to get to me." He screamed.

"I can fix this Gary." I said trying to calm him down.

"What? How the hell you gonna fix it? Girl get hell out the freaking house now."

"Gary I can make a new batch before they get here."

"What? Lana you don't know nothing about cheffin up. "

"Yes I do cuzzo. I be watching you on the low all the time. I know the right measurements and everything Gary."

"Man hell no. Now get outta there. I aint gonna say it again." He barked.

"Look Cuzzo as much as you've done for me I aint about to let nothing happen to you. Get home when you can and all will be well." I said before I hung up the phone.

I hung up the phone and moved through the house like greased lightning gathering everything I needed to save both of our lives. Within minutes I was in the kitchen at the stove praying out loud.

"Dear God I know I shouldn't be asking for nothing like this, but please let me get this right."

I said a hail Mary, crossed my heart and began to whoop up that work. It's a good thing I wasn't actually cooking food because I was sweating nervously all up in the pot.

"C'mon Lana you got this. Not too much baking soda. Okay now bring it back baby." I kept saying out loud to myself as my eyes kept shifting from the clock back to the pot.

I tried to use my photogenic to the best of my ability and hoped that I was completing the last step correctly.

"Okay now Lana. Weigh it wet for maximum profit." I coached myself.

There was a knock at the door on queue as I packaged up the last of the work, said one more prayer and headed for the door.

"Wassup Shorty? Where Gary at?" D-Boy said pushing passed me while his crack testing fiend followed him into the house.

"He aint here and you can't just come all up in here like that." I snapped.

"Shut up. That nigga got my money so I'll do what I want." He replied with a stare that confirmed he would hurt me if I didn't make something shake really quick.

"He got tied up, but I got what you need. Follow me." I said leading them into the kitchen.

When we got in the kitchen I handed over the product.

"What you just standing there for? Break a piece off and fire that work up." He said slapping the fiend across the face.

The terrified fiend did as she was told as she broke a piece of the rock off, put it into her stem, and lit the pipe.

"This shit better be right or we gonna have a problem up in here." D-Boy said pulling his gun out of his waistline.

I waited nervously as it seemed like forever before my work was graded by the smoker although it was only 5 seconds that had passed.

"This is the best batch ever." She said as she exhaled the smoke and her eyes rolled into the back of her head.

My heart finally started beating at a normal pace.

"Tell Gary I said whatever he did to this batch he needs to do to all of the work from now on."

"No doubt. I'll let him know." I said pushing the work across the table to him.

"Hold up. I aint order all of this. This is way too much." He snapped.

Damn I never even asked Gary how big the order was.

"It's cool. If it's as good as Brenda here says it is I'll take it all." He said pulling a wad of money out of his pocket and peeling off 5 thousand dollars.

He took what was left of the drugs and left just as quickly as he had come. And I was tripping because it seemed like as soon as he left Gary came busting through the door.

"Lana. Yo Lana where you at cuz?" He yelled frantically running through the house obviously imagining the worst.

"Whoa! Whoa! Slow down. I'm right here." I said stepping out of the kitchen.

"Are you okay? I just saw D-Boy pull off." He asked giving me the once over.

"Yes cuz I'm okay and everything is all good." I said trying to calm him down.

"What do you mean everything is all good? What happened?"

I didn't say anything I just handed him the five thousand dollars.

"Hold up. What's this?" he asked visibly shocked.

"I told you I handled the situation. I not only took care of his order but he said it was so good that he bought everything you had left in the stash. He also said that whatever you did to this batch he wants done to 'em all from now on."

"Yoooo what did you do?" he asked overjoyed as he picked me up and swung me around.

"I looked out for family like I was supposed to." I said proudly.

CHAPTER 5

After coming through in the clutch for Gary he altered the house rules a little bit. I still had to go to school and get straight A's, and I still had to stay away from boys, but now I was in charge of cooking up all of the drugs for Gary. We had a good thing going; I would cook up the drugs and Gary would sell them. We had the best product in the hood and because of that Gary was the new supplier that everyone was coming to.

The family business was booming and we were both living it up. I was making nowhere near the money Gary was making, but the money he was paying me to cook up was damn good. I stayed in all the flyest gear, jewelry, and hair, and I never wanted for anything. I was admiring a new outfit I had just bought when Gary called.

"Get dressed. You been working hard, it's time to have some fun; we going out."

"Sounds fun, but it's a school night Gary." I said reminding him.

"It's cool. You can take a day off; you earned it. I'll be there to pick you up in an hour."

I can't even lie, I was super hyped up about going out so I pulled out one of my dopest outfits and got ready. When Gary pulled up he blew the horn and I rushed out the house and into the passenger seat of his brand new 5 series BMW.

"So where are we going, to the movies or something?" I asked curiously.

"The movies? Hell nah we bout to hit the Blue Room. I already reserved us a lil V.I.P. booth."

"The Blue Room? You know I'm way too young to get up in there. I said suddenly bummed out because the Blue Room is where all of the money making drug dealers and high end women went to party.

"#1 you don't look 14 and #2 you with me so you good." He said pulling off.

When we pulled up to the club the sidewalk and parking lot was packed like Wal-Mart on Black Friday.

"Daaaaaamn. Look at that line and where we gonna park? I hope the line moves fast or these heels gonna tear my feet up." I said dreading the wait.

"Lil cuz we park in valet and we don't stand in no lines." Gary said pulling up to the front door and handing the valet the keys as we got out of the car.

As the bouncer unhooked the rust metal chain and allowed us to skip the never ending line the men's mouths were watering as my 14-year-old soul filled out my 25-year-old dress. The women in line gave just the opposite look as they wore hate all on their faces.

That night there were more stars in the club than there were in the sky. Everybody who was anybody was there popping bottles and throwing tons of money in the air. I was in Heaven.

"Drink up. This stuff is too expensive to go to waste." Gary said referencing the two magnum bottles of liquor he had purchased.

I did as I was told and partied like it was my last day on Earth. I was drinking, dancing, and throwing money in the air like everybody else. I was also attracting a lot of attention while Gary warded off all of the grown men that were flocking my way.

I was so drunk I don't even remember leaving the club or the ride home. I vaguely remember stumbling up the front steps to the doorway while Gary laughed and held me up.

"C'mon lightweight I got you." Gary said unable to control his laughter while guiding me through the door and into the house.

"Big Cuz thanks for taking me out. I really had the time of my life." I said slurring my words uncontrollably.

"It's all good. You deserved it and you earned it." He said leading me upstairs to my bedroom.

"I'm gonna take a shower and go to bed. I'mma set my alarm and try to get up and go to school too." I said meaning every word of it.

"I seriously doubt you gonna make it to school, but I give you and "A" for effort. Good night lil Cuz." He said as he headed to his room.

I went in my room and immediately took all of my clothes off. I smelled like liquor, sweat, and smoke and it was making me nauseous. After getting undressed I grabbed my towel, nightclothes etc. and headed into the shower.

I seriously hoped that the steam and hot water would sober me up, but for some reason it did the total opposite. I wasn't in the shower a full 5 minutes before the room started spinning and I went crashing down into the tub pulling the shower curtain, and soap valet down with me. The noise brought Gary running in to save the day.

"What the hell happened?" he said.

"Sorry I broke ya curtains cuz." Was all I could say, I was totally out of it.

"I aint worried about them curtains. I'm worried about you." He said lifting me up out of the tub and carrying me back to my bedroom.

"You lay right here I'll be right back." He said as he disappeared out of the room.

Within seconds he was back with an iced cold rag and applying it to my forehead.

"Here you go lil cuz. Just lay back and relax." He said.

"Thanks for taking care of me Gary." I said weakly and barley able to finish the sentence.

"Come on now, we family. We supposed to take care of each other."

That was the last thing I heard him say before I passed out. Thank God for Gary.

****
****

While I was sleeping I kept feeling drops of water hitting me. If this was Gary's way of waking me up for school it was annoying as hell. I was still drunk and still couldn't get my bearings.

"Chill cuz." I said as I opened my eyes to find out that the water was actually sweat pouring from Gary's face as he stood over me pumping away at his private and watching me in a way that was all too familiar. I was too weak to fight; I could only plead as the Hennessy filled tears fell from my eyes.

"Garry please stop. We family." I cried.

"I'm sorry but after seeing you tonight I can see why Jason did what he did to you."

I couldn't believe what was happening. My hero, had turned into the big bad wolf that he had once saved me from right before my eyes.

"You aint no different from Jason." I cried.

"No sweetheart. That's where you're wrong; Jason was a sick pervert, I'm nothing like him."

The look in his eyes said he was passionate and sincere and that's what scared me the most. I just laid there crying as he walked out smiling. Morning couldn't come soon enough.

CHAPTER 6

I woke up the next morning even more creeped out as Gary stood there with his arms crossed, watching me like a damn soap opera. I was two hours late for school but I didn't care. I climbed out from under the comforters that shielded my body, threw on anything I could find, and left for school. I was so distraught I didn't bathe, brush my teeth, do my hair or nothing. I just wanted to get out of the house and school was the only place I get safe at this point.

I was in such a disoriented daze on my way to school I don't even remember the 18 minute walk. What I do remember are the looks, points, and whispers as I stumbled down the hall towards my 3rd period class. When I got there the door was locked so I had to knock and interrupt the class. The look on Mrs. Bailey's face said it all as she headed to the door.

"Nice of you to join us Lana." She said semi-sarcastically as she opened the door.

I was never late and I got the highest grades in her class so she wasn't really tripping. Again with the looks, points, and whispers as I made my way to my desk.

"Okay class. Now where were we?" Mrs. Bailey said picking up where she left off.

About 20 minutes into class I found myself in deep thought, haunted by all things I have experienced, and all the pain I have endured. I then heard a blood curdling scream. As expected it startled everyone. It startled me the most to find out it was coming from me. I had totally lost it; last night's events had driven me over the edge. Today was not going to be a school day so I left.

After walking around aimlessly for hours, I came to the harsh reality that I truly had no place to go. I no longer trusted Gary; how could I? Before I knew it I was back in front of Granny's house. I stood there for a long while looking at the front door checking and double checking my other options. I mean you have to remember, this place had so many horrid memories that I didn't want to relive.

"God please give me a sign." I said out loud and magically I could feel a force pushing me towards the door.

I took my keys out, opened it, and let myself in. the place seemed to be empty. I assumed my siblings were at school, and my grandparents were doing their work down at the church. I was glad no one was home. All I wanted to do was take a shower, lie down, relax, and figure out a way to choke on my pride and ask to come home.

I made my way through the house and up the stairs when I heard noises coming from upstairs. I slowed down my pace because I wanted to be clear of what the noises were. Apparently Jason was home and he had company. His bedroom door was cracked, so I could see the girl being pleased by my brother, which was no big deal, but I was just sick of it all. I had seen the sign that God had shown me; this was not the place for me. I quietly made my way back down the steps and out of the house. Once outside I ran as fast as I could with no particular destination in mind. I was crying so hard my vision mirrored that of driving through a rainstorm. "God, I really need you, the pain is becoming unbearable. Why would anyone want to go through this? I'm only a child, yet I've lost my childhood. I'm tired of the people that's supposed to love, end up hurting me the most. Where is my happiness? When will the pain stop? Are you even listening?" I was convinced God wasn't listening to me. This wasn't my first time praying. I have prayed many times before, especially during every sexual attack, but they never stopped. I feel like God is letting this happen to me. But, why me? This can't be life I thought to myself. The sound of a car horn broke my trance as I almost ran into the middle of traffic. Looking around, thinking what I should do next, I quickly realized that at this point, I only had one other place I could go.

I got to my mom's house and turned the knob knowing the door would be open; it was always open. It was no surprise to me that the house was filthy and smelled like mildew and crack smoke. I followed the trail of putrid smoke to the kitchen where my mother and a very large man sat at the table passing a Budweiser back and forth as if they were both dying of thirst. Although I hadn't seen my mother in what seemed like years she acknowledged me like she had just saw me the night before.

"Lana this is Smallz. Smallz this is Lana." She said eyes half closed.

"This big nigga name is Smallz?" I thought to myself as I laughed inside.

"Go on and make yourself a plate." My mother said nodding towards the food on the stove that about 15 roaches had already beaten me to.

"Um nah. I'm good. Look I'm coming back home; if that's okay." I said not knowing what her answer would be.

"Of course you can come home baby. Your room is just the way you left it. Oh, and Dana has moved back here to, so you both are sharing a room. You won't see her much though because she is always in the streets. "She took a sip of the Budweiser and then passed it back to Smallz. "I haven't even seen her since she moved back in. I only know she has been here from the sweet smelling body wash that lingers around in the bathroom making me sick to my stomach" my mother said as she held her stomach with her face twisted up, as if she was becoming nauseous just thinking about it.

"Okay well I'm going to go and get some sleep. It's been a long night." I said feeling drained.

"Yeah okay. Hey, you got any money on you?" She asked taking a large hit of the crack filled blunt she was trying to hide, but failed tremendously.

"No ma. I'm broke sorry." I lied as I turned and headed towards my room.

As I was walking away I heard something that almost made me double back and spaz out.

"Yo. Why you tell her she could move in here?" Smallz asked seemingly frustrated.

I was waiting for my mother to come to my defense. And I'm still waiting.

"Shut the hell up. I need to add her to my welfare so we can get more food stamps and money stupid."

Like I said, I wanted to spaz out, but knew that I had no place else to go so I let it ride.

CHAPTER 7

Over the next few weeks I once again endured the pain and suffering of living with an addict for a mother. All her and Smallz did was sit around playing Tunk, and getting high all day. They had damn near sold all of the foodstamps to support their habits so I thought it was wise that I hid my money in a hole in the wall in my room. I only hoped that the rats wouldn't eat it before I had a chance to spend it.

Even though I was living in such horrid conditions I still went to school every day and bust those books out. Somehow deep down inside school was therapeutic and an escape from my everyday reality. Jason had been blowing up my trap phone, but I kept ignoring him. The situation was so weird I had no idea why he kept calling me. His voicemails just kept telling me to either call or come by, but that was never gonna happen.

Things at home were getting worse. My mother was starting to be away from the house more and more leaving me alone with Smallz. The way he looked at me made me very uncomfortable. Many of nights I begged my mom not to leave me alone with him, but the cry of the drugs was apparently much louder than that of her child.

After seeing my mother come in at the wee hours of the morning and handing wads of cash over to Smallz I quickly surmised that after there was nothing left to sell in the house to sell, so she had to get money for the only thing in the house that still had a little value left to it; her jewelry. Normally, that's the first thing that goes with addicts, but my mother was very protective over he jewelry. I mean she would wear all her jewelry at one time, and would let anyone touch it or wear it. If that wasn't bad enough they were blowing the money on drugs instead of paying for the lights, gas, and food. It's a good thing that due to Section 8 our rent was only $68.00, and even then, they were late with that at times.

I couldn't stand staying here. I mean they wouldn't just get high in front of me, but I wasn't stupid. My mother was so far gone that I could be gone for weeks at a time staying with classmates or whoever just to get away and she wouldn't even come looking for me. The sad thing is I don't even know if she realized I was even gone all that time.

As time went on the weather started to change and as you can probably imagine the heat and hot water were turned off. I still haven't seen my sister much; she was considered a run away my mother said. I haven't smelled that sweet body wash that she uses in that bathroom lately, so I know she hasn't been by. Dana grew up to be real tough, she didn't mind fighting, and with no words at all, she would do just that. I missed Dana, but I knew she was tired of this life too. I always we had a stronger relationship and that she will at least come to see me, but that's the least of the concerns that I need God to address. My mother was still "working" at night and leaving me alone with Smallz fat sloppy self. Tonight I was asleep after a long night of studying. I was shivering and the tattered quilt that had been on my bed since forever was doing me no justice. It was almost impossible to sleep as I could see my breath in the air with each exhale. I had never uttered two words to Smallz the whole time I had been there, but tonight I had to swallow my pride. I walked into my mother's room where he was sitting in dented in recliner while watching the Arsenio Hall Show.

"Excuse me Mr. Smallz. Are there any spare blankets around here?"

His eyes rolled into the back of his head as I interrupted him on the treadmill or something.

"Nah. Aint no more. Now go to bed." He snapped as he stretched out, leaned back and slipped his hands into a pants.

I silently cursed him and went back to my bedroom.

I was lying in my bed crying as tears that never made it to my cheek froze solid right under my eyes. I had finally cried myself to sleep when I suddenly felt heat take over my room. Before I knew what was going on Smallz had his fat, hairy, smelly arms standing in my room.

"Come clean the dishes" he said sounding as if he just ran a marathon

"Schmmp" I sucked my teeth and jumped out of the bed. I through my long black bubble coat because it was even colder in the kitchen. I don't know how the hell I was going to clean dishes with cold water. Welp! I wasn't eating off of them so it didn't matter. I stood at the sink and tried to get this over with quickly, I just wanted to be back in my room and away from Smallz.

"I know you're cold, but don't worry darling, Smallz gonna keep you warm." He said coming up behind me fondling my breast through my coat while grinding against me.

At this point in my life I was convinced that this was just supposed to be happening to me; so once again I just stood there and took it. Here this fat monster was molesting me and I didn't say a word or fight back. Within seconds Smallz let out a loud grunt and whispered in my ear.

"He's lying ma I swear." I said as I hurled the pot at Smallz and beaned him right in his head causing it to split open and gush blood everywhere."

"Is this how you show your appreciation to Smallz after he let you come and live in my house?

Yeah ya'll read it right. I couldn't believe what I was hearing.

"Mama, Smallz is the one that be in my grinding on me almost every day touching me and sticking his tongue in my mouth." I cried.

"Oh now you gonna lie on my man?"

"Ma I swear I aint lying." I screamed.

"What do Smallz want with a little girl when he got all this woman right here?" she said running her hand over her frail body.

"If she gonna be here I gotta go." Smallz said.

"No baby, don't go; Lana I'm sorry, but you can't go around lying like that." She screamed at me.

Again, I couldn't believe what was coming out of her mouth.

"What? You gonna choose him over me?"

"You shouldn't have been so hot in the ass." She screamed.

"You always put that man before your kids. What type of mother does that? You know what don't answer that. You don't have to say anything more, I'm leaving!"

At this point she didn't have to tell me again. I ran upstairs, grabbed as much as I could carry and headed for the front door. I slowed down as I approached the door and turned around hoping she would realize that I was only 14 with nowhere to go, but instead all she was doing was caressing Smallz.

"Don't worry baby. She gone and aint coming back."

That was the last thing I heard before leaving and slamming the screen door so hard that it shattered the glass. I wandered the streets for hours taking breaks when I could while trying to figure things out. One thing for sure and two things for certain I was never gonna return to any of the places that I had left.

CHAPTER 8

Over the next couple of months I went from house to house staying with whatever classmates would let me crash temporarily. Through it all I was still doing my thing in school. I was getting into a few arguments and petty beefs over people making jokes about my living situation and the fact that I was often wearing the same thing over and over again. For the most part I ignored the B.S. but then people started getting really disrespectful. I found myself fighting almost every day taking out my aggressions on any and everybody who crossed me or pissed me off. I eventually made a name for myself, as everyone started calling me "Lady or Lil ALI." I wouldn't start fights, but that didn't mean I didn't know how to fight. I was slick with the hands and they came quick too.

My teachers all knew something was going on with me, because this fighting and carrying on was not me. I was slowly but surely transforming into someone that I wasn't, but I felt it necessary to survive this life that I had been given. I had started drinking, smoking, and hanging out all times of night. I was becoming Dana who was 100% ten toes down in the streets. She had already been in and out of the juvenile detention center. She had even gotten so bad that she did time in the County jail even though she was still a minor. Dana had started gang banging and was well respected in the streets. I can't go into what she did and is responsible for, but just know that even adults wouldn't cross her. I didn't want to become Dana by any stretch of the imagination. As I stated before we were total opposites, but lately I was not too far removed from who she was and I wasn't feeling it.

It wasn't long before I had worn out my welcome at all of the places I had been staying. I was finally out of options so I turned to the only thing besides school that I knew how to do well. I rented a room in a boarding house full of crackheads and I started selling drugs right there to the residents, and while the living conditions were poor as always the money I was making hand over fist all but made up for it. I had to lie about my age to the landlord as well as all of the tenants. I didn't look 15 so it wasn't an issue.

Before long I had saved up enough money to get me new clothes, a new look, and a new crib. Once again I would have to lie about my age in order to get it, and once again that wasn't a problem. By this time I had damn near completely transformed into totally different person. My new job as a drug dealer had gained me some new associates. Looking back, I knew they were all nothing but bad elements, but in this game you needed allies; you needed a crew.

I had started dating a man named David. He wasn't from my area, but would come and buy drugs from me. Nah he wasn't a fiend, he just knew I had the best product around so he would come buy from me and then go back to his hood and make a killing. For some reason I had told David my real age one of the many times he tried to hit on me. I figured it would serve as a deterrent, but it seemed to only further excite the 22-year-old dope boy. Although there was a 7-year age difference and it was technically illegal, David made sense when he told me that in my line of work I needed a man to protect me and hold me down. That, coupled with the fact that he was well connected and looked hella good sold me on the idea of us being this ghetto power couple. I have to admit that David and I were making noise in the streets with our little situation. With the product I was whipping up David was the man on his side of town and I was the HBIC on my side.

I can't front David had me open and I would follow him to the ends of the earth. He was teaching me things about the streets that I had never known or seen. He taught me all about guns; how to shoot, clean, and handle them. At first I told him that I didn't like guns, but he assured me that I would need to deal with them if I was gonna be in this life. So I did what my man wanted me to do, and always did.

One Friday we were at my house having a get together. It was me, David, and some locals from around my way. Everyone was drinking, smoking, gambling, and having a good time. I had gone upstairs to get some more weed from out of my stash when I was approached by a local hustler named Lil Maniac.

"Yo. What that nigga doing here?" He said referring to David.

"That's my man. What you mean what he doing here?" I snapped.

"That nigga robbed me and my man the other day."

"Nah you bugging. That aint possible cuz he aint even from around here." I said arguing the lies Lil Maniac was telling.

"Man I know who robbed me. Now you know who I am and you also know my brother Big Maniac, so you already know what it is. I'm about to teach you about riding with the wrong niggas." He said as he pulled a sawed off shotgun out of his pants.

"Yo. What are you doing?" I said fearing the worst.

they were all nothing but bad elements, but in this game you needed allies; you needed a crew.

I had started dating a man named David. He wasn't from my area, but would come and buy drugs from me. Nah he wasn't a fiend, he just knew I had the best product around so he would come buy from me and then go back to his hood and make a killing. For some reason I had told David my real age one of the many times he tried to hit on me. I figured it would serve as a deterrent, but it seemed to only further excite the 22-year-old dope boy. Although there was a 7-year age difference and it was technically illegal, David made sense when he told me that in my line of work I needed a man to protect me and hold me down. That, coupled with the fact that he was well connected and looked hella good sold me on the idea of us being this ghetto power couple. I have to admit that David and I were making noise in the streets with our little situation. With the product I was whipping up David was the man on his side of town and I was the HBIC on my side.

I can't front David had me open and I would follow him to the ends of the earth. He was teaching me things about the streets that I had never known or seen. He taught me all about guns; how to shoot, clean, and handle them. At first I told him that I didn't like guns, but he assured me that I would need

to deal with them if I was gonna be in this life. So I did what my man wanted me to do, and always did.

One Friday we were at my house having a get together. It was me, David, and some locals from around my way. Everyone was drinking, smoking, gambling, and having a good time. I had gone upstairs to get some more weed from out of my stash when I was approached by a local hustler named Lil Maniac.

"Yo. What that nigga doing here?" He said referring to David.

"That's my man. What you mean what he doing here?" I snapped.

"That nigga robbed me and my man the other day."

"Nah you bugging. That aint possible cuz he aint even from around here." I said arguing the lies Lil Maniac was telling.

"Man I know who robbed me. Now you know who I am and you also know my brother Big Maniac, so you already know what it is. I'm about to teach you about riding with the wrong niggas." He said as he pulled a sawed off shotgun out of his pants.

"Yo. What are you doing?" I said fearing the worst.

"You either gonna get down or lay down." He said pulling me in the open closet and raping me right there on the spot.

I opened my mouth to scream for David and he stuck the barrel of the gun in it.

"Try it and Imma blast yo ass. Now shut up and take it." He said taking what little innocence I had left away from me.

I don't recall how long the rape went on, but what I do know is that nobody came looking for me. Besides the fact that I was being raped in a house full of people I was bugging off the fact that David never even came to check on me once he saw that me and Lil Maniac were gone. I mean what kind of man would do something like that. It wasn't until the ordeal was over that David got up to come and look for me. Lil Maniac had finished his business with me and left the room. Minutes later David came in.

"Hey where you been?" he said with a dumb look on his face.

I didn't even respond. I just walked past him and headed back to the party as if nothing ever happened. That was my last time seeing or speaking to David. After the mess he pulled I wanted no parts of him. At this point I thought he was either in on it or just too dumb to know that his girl was being raped by another man right under his nose; either way he was not the man for me. So I broke things off and told him if I ever saw him again I would show him just how much I was paying attention during his weapons training. He never confirmed or denied, he just never came back.

CHAPTER 9

After the fiasco with Lil Maniac I went back to business as usual. I had to hustle to survive and there was no way around it. I figured I only had to do this until I got out of school then I would go away to college and leave all of these nightmares behind me.

I was walking home from school and my eyes got as big as the moon when I approached my house and saw police tape and cops all around it.

"What's going on here?" I asked the cop that was closest to me.

"Why? Do you live here?" He asked.

"No but my friend does; and I'm worried about her." I lied.

"Well the bad news is the place was sprayed with bullets, vandalized, and robbed. The good news is nobody was home when it happened. Who's your friend?" He said as I turned and high tailed it up the block.

Rule #1 never talk to the cops.

****
****

I had to go chill at a friend's house until the chaos at my house subsided. All I kept thinking all day is *"who would shoot my crib up?"* and I hope they didn't find my stash because if they did I was totally screwed. I waited for night fall and hurried back to my house. By now the police were gone and it was just the local neighborhood crew hanging out. Of course no one saw what happened but I didn't care all I wanted was my money so I could move once again, because obviously this house was no longer safe for me.

I lifted the yellow police caution tape, let myself into my house and immediately thanked God that I wasn't home when this all went down. I looked at the bullet riddled walls of my now ransacked house and I started to become angry. No matter where I go or what I do, I just can't get a break. Am I being punished for something? Is this really what life is about, pain, struggle and torment? I checked stash spot # 1 and all of my drugs were gone. I ran upstairs and checked stash spot #2 which was a hole in my mattress that I filled with money and covered with the filling from the mattress. I counted the money and it was all there. Once again I grabbed as much of my things as I could carry and I left before whoever did this came back to finish what they started.

I stayed at a hotel for a while until I could find another place to live. I made sure the hotel was close to school because believe it or not I still loved school and my grades reelected as such. In a week or so I found a new place that wasn't too far away; it was actually just two towns over. I decided to go that route as to not see the same faces everyday especially after what had happened. So once again it was a fresh start, but with each fresh start I started losing myself piece by piece.

I was in school one day and a friend of mine was arguing with some girl. The argument had nothing to do with me, yet it was irritating me to no end. The fact that they were both just doing a bunch of talk and showing no action was really pissing me off. I know I was just angry about all that I have been through, but I was just ready to hit to the both of them.

"Yo what's popping Kisha, if you don't punch this broad in the face so we can go." I barked at my friend.

"She aint about to do nothing. She either gonna get down or lay down." The girl fired back.

That phrase brought back flashbacks of the rape by lil Maniac and I blacked out. I jumped on the girl and beat her so bad she had to be hospitalized. I swole both eyes, broke her nose, and knocked a few teeth out. All of that accompanied by a stage 2 concussion.

Shockingly there were no charges filed, but the school had had enough. I was kicked out of school and that really hurt more than anything. I tried to get into other schools, but my reputation had now preceded me and I was denied everywhere I went, except night school. Who wants to go to school at night? This thing called life was just getting worse.

CHAPTER 10

After being kicked out of school things just spiraled downward from there. The drug game had dried up for me, and with no money I was once again put out of my house. I was literally scraping the bottom of the barrel at that point. I started going to church, but spiritually I was dead. I even stayed with a few church members. They knew just bits and pieces of what I was going through, but not enough to cause change. Some of the kids in the church even talked about me, my clothes or the way I smelled. They had no idea what it was like living in my shoes, and I left it to their imagination.

Just thinking about everything, once again the pain began to succumb me. I fell on my knees and I started crying dreadfully, tears soaking up my face as if I was standing in the middle of a rain storm, and if I was, I was crying so hard I wouldn't be able to tell the difference between the rain drops and my tears. All the pain came rushing at once and I just started to scream out, praying…

"God… many times I have prayed silently and out loud. I really don't know if you are listening, can you hear me? They say you are always there when we call, but it feels like I'm leaving message after message. I don't want to be here anymore; I want to die! I'm tired of being hurt, why do you keep allowing this to happen to me. You're

Alpha and Omega, and you have the strength and power to stop this but you won't. Time after time I have been violated. Time after time I have called you. Time after time I have been abused, and time after time you have not answered. Where are you God, why won't you save me. I don't know what to do, who to go to, or what to say."

Still crying and screaming, I looked down at myself and continued to pray,

"I'm hungry, I'm filthy, I'm hurting God. What have I done to deserve this, what have I done to deserve all this pain! Why doesn't anyone love me, all they do is hurt me. I just want to die; I just want to diiieeee!"

I continued to scream,

"I can't take it anymore! Save me God, help me God, take the pain away God, please! Why aren't you saying anything……"

I sat there soaked in tears still on my knees for about 15 minutes, just hoping to hear his voice, hoping that he will send a sign, wishing he would come and save me. But no one came, I saw no signs, and regardless of how quiet it was, I did not hear his voice...I was lost

I was at my wits end and seemingly left for dead when out of nowhere I got a premonition. I suddenly remembered that I had an aunt that lived out of town. I rummaged through my belongings and found her phone number with hopes that it was still the same since I hadn't spoken to her in years. I gave her a call and explained all that I had been through (well most of it) and she told me that as long as I could get to her she would let me live with her. She lived a few cities over so I just needed to hustle up the travel money. That phone call gave me a sigh of relief and a ray of hope. I thanked God that he gave me the notion to remember my aunt and to make that call. I would get the bus money, move to another city and start over yet again, but this time would be the real deal. No more selling drugs, no more fights, and I would finally finish school.

I wasn't able to get the bus money up, so I walk which took a matter of hours. I was so hype about the trip that I put my hustle in overdrive to make it happen. The walk seemed like it took forever, but when I reached my destination it felt like my soul was in a whole 'nother body.

When I got there my Aunt Julie welcomed me with opened arms. We laughed and talked as I filled her in on this hell that had become my life.

"Well I just wanna tell you things are different down here." She said as we walked back to her house from the corner she met me on.

"Different how?" I asked.

"Oh you'll see. You gonna have to get adjusted real fast."

"Trust me. That's all I have been doing over the years. Adjusting is no problem." I said as we both shared a laugh.

Within minutes we walked up to my aunts gated community

"Auntie must be doin aight for herself." I said to myself as she entered the gate code and we watched them open automatically.

We pulled into the complex and I immediately had a change of perception as the gates closed behind us and the residents swarmed the courtyard like roaches. There were babies running around with nothing on but pampers, hoodrats with bright multi-colored hair extensions, and what appeared to be a sea of Blood Gang affiliates flagging and flying their colors any way they saw fit. It was then that I realized that the gate was not to keep bad element out, but more so to keep the bad element in.

****
****

I had only been at my Aunt's for a few days before that whole adjustment thing needed to be kicked in. As it turned out my Aunt was struggling as well. She wasn't on drugs, but work became hard to find so was pigeonholed into living a sub-standard lifestyle. That didn't matter though! I would do anything for my aunt because she opened her doors for me when she didn't have to. My aunt was my new best-friend.

About a few months after being there I was on my way back from the store when I was approached by a group of girls I had seen around the complex.

"Waddup bruh?" Queenie said as she stepped in front of me while the others surrounded me.

"Excuse me?" I asked naively

"You the new broad in the gates aint you? Who you affiliated with?"

"Huh? Nobody. I came to stay with my aunt." Lawd I was dumb.

"Yeah well that aint gonna cut it." She said pulling a razor out from under her tongue.

"Look I don't want no problems." I said trying to avoid an altercation. I knew my hands were on point, but I never had to use weapons.

"Yeah well around here you gonna need friends. We don't allow no strays in the gates.

"I'm cool." I said trying to walk past.

"Nah. No you aint." Queenie said as she gave the signal.

The punches and kicks seemed to be coming a mile a minute from every direction.

"So this is what an ass whooping feels like." I thought to myself as I covered up and tried to absorb as a many of the blows as possible.

It seemed like the beating took hours when in all actuality it was only three minutes.

Queenie gave the signal for the beating to cease just as she had given it to begin.

"Pick the hoe up." She instructed as her minions did her bidding.

I stood to my feet bleeding from my mouth and nose.

"Now this can be a one and done thing if you fall in line or we can do this every time we see you. Now I'm gon' ask you one more time; who you rolling with?"

With no fear I looked Queenie dead in the eye and responded.

"Almighty Blood Nation" thinking to myself, what in the world did I just do? It was better than getting jumped, so I guess.

CHAPTER 11

Life was different when I became a member of the Bloods. I mean we were steady mobbing. When you saw one of us you saw dozens of us. My aunt didn't like the life I was living, but she aint complain too much because I was making sure that we never wanted for anything. I was back to selling drugs again and making even more money than before.

I was also known for my A1 fight game. I was tall, pretty, sexy and not to be messed with. You guys are probably not gonna believe this but through all of my gangbanging, and weed smoking I still went to school at night and graduated, so I thought. With all of the negative I had in my life I needed something positive and getting my diploma was the shining moment I needed. After getting my diploma I had a feeling of accomplishment. I finally started feeling a sense of purpose in my life, and although it was only a piece of paper it was the fight to get that diploma that urged me to change my life around.

I had started weaning myself away from Queenie and the rest of the crew slowly. I knew the consequences that could bring, but I didn't care. Who knew that getting my diploma would trigger such an inner piece within me? In any event I stopped selling drugs, and focused on getting a real job. My aunt was kind of on the fence about my decision to quit because although it meant me being safe and out of harm's way it also meant a change in our financial situation at home. We both agreed it was a good trade off so she supported me. She supported me in everything that I did. She was the only one that showed unconditional love. With her raising three kids though, I knew I couldn't stay with her too much longer. I was becoming a burden, and would soon have to find other resources. At least that's how I felt.

My change didn't only come in the streets. I had decided to make a major life change my switching religions. I felt that all the bad stuff I had been through happened under the cover of Christianity so fully converted to the Muslim faith. When I say fully, I mean fully. I totally committed myself; I gave up Coogie, and other designers for pure Muslim garb complete with headdress. Once Queenie and the rest saw me make that move they shockingly accepted it and let me be.

****
****

There was a new fish and wing spot that opened up across the street from the complex that everybody was making a big deal about. I never really went over there because I was almost positive that they cooked pork and beef in the same oil and my new found faith wouldn't allow that type of cross contamination. I was sitting at the kitchen table studying the Quran when auntie asked me to walk across the street to the food spot with her.

"C'mon Auntie. I don't feel like going over there I'm studying right now."

"Girl come take a walk with me. Allah will understand trust me." She joked.

I knew she wasn't gonna give up so I just placed a book marker in the Quran, closed it and reluctantly took the walk with her.

When we walked into the spot I instantly felt glad that I had taken the walk with her. The man behind the counter had my heart beating out of my chest. He was tall, muscular, long flowing frosted locks, tattoos, and eyes that would melt any woman's heart. The whole time Auntie was ordering her food I discreetly stared at the owner.

"C'mon let's go." Auntie said snapping me out of my trance.

She was babbling about something all the way back to the house, but I was in my own zone contemplating my next move.

"Hey auntie do they make salads over there?"

"Yeah girl; they good too."

"Okay I'll be back. I'mma run over and grab one."

"Want me to walk back over with you?"

"No. You sit down and eat before ya food gets cold. I'll be right back." I said as I dashed out of the house before she could insist on coming with me.

I got across the street in record time, composed myself, caught my breath and entered the store. When I locked eyes with him, my salad story went right out the window.

"Hi. I'm Lana take my number." I said boldly.

"Hey Lana I'm Kwazi." He said handing me a pen and paper.

I was so nervous that my hand was shaking as I wrote my cell number down.

"Here you go." I said sliding it back to him.

"You Muslim?" He asked stupidly.

"What on earth gave it away the headdress and full garb?" I responded sarcastically while smiling flirtatiously and leaving.

From that day forth Kwazi and I were inseparable.

CHAPTER 12

About a month after Kwazi and I started dating I moved out of my aunt's house and in with a friend I had met while working for a temp agency. I figured out of respect for my aunt I wasn't gonna be laid up with my man so my friend said I could come and stay with her. This way I had my own room and could do whatever I want with whomever I wanted to do it with. After a few months of staying with Karen, Kwazi and I decided it was time for us to get our own place together. We both knew that this is what we wanted so that we could continue to be happy together. I mean without any exaggeration Kwazi was everything I ever wanted and needed in a man, and despite the huge age difference we were in love and happy. Kwazi treated me like royalty, and I returned the gesture daily.

Kwazi and I had finally settled on the house we wanted. Once the realtor gave us the amount we needed to move in we decided that I would pay half of the deposit and he would cover the other half. It would take some saving on both of our ends but we knew we could do it because it's what we wanted.

After saving for what seemed like forever I was ready to make the down payment. On the way home from work I was so happy I could barely keep my composure. I called Kwazi to inform him of the good news.

"Hello?" He said as he answered.

"Hey baby guess what?"

"Wassup?"

"With what I got paid today I have my half of the move in costs for the new house. Meet me over there with your half so we can sign the paperwork and get the keys." I said excitedly.

"Yeah look about that." He said somberly.

"Oh lord this man done dipped into the money, but no biggie I will just replace it with what I have." I thought to myself.

"Wassup baby talk to me."

"This aint gonna work Lana."

"What? You changed ya mind about the house? Okay no problem we will find another one that's all."

"No Lana it's us; we aint gonna work." He said as cold as he could.

My heart sank into my draws. I just knew I was being punked and was waiting on that white boy to jump out with a camera crew, but he never came.

"Kwazi what are you talking about? I love you baby. Where is all of this coming from? I said with tears in my eyes.

"It been on my mind for a while now. You just too young for me and the age difference is starting to show in your actions. Look I don't wanna make this a long drawn out thing. Just know we need to end it."

My hurt suddenly turned to anger.

"Word? That's how you feel? Aight then deuces." I said as I was about to hang up.

"Lana wait a minute."

Yeah that's what I thought. I said to myself poking my chest out.

"What Kwazi?"

"I need that money you got."

Now I really thought I was being punked. That nigga had bumped his head.

"Excuse me nigga? What did you say?"

I knew I was heated because I had not used the word nigga since I converted to Islam.

"I need that money we were gonna use to move in. I gotta bust a move. I'mma flip it and give you double back." He said almost pleading for the cash.

"Kwazi you got me all the way messed up. Good bye." I said as I hung up the phone.

I had decided to get all of my crying out before I got back to Karen's house because I wasn't ready to tell her what happened because I knew if I did she was gonna wanna talk about it and I damn sure wasn't in the mood. So I just went home, took a nice hot shower and cried myself to sleep in my room.

The next morning I was off so I decided to blow off some steam by going for a nice long run so I grabbed my iPod and headed out. The whole time I was running I was listening to nothing but mood music. Mobb Deep, Lil Kim, Biggie, Tupac, Wu-Tang etc. I believe I ran about 4 or 5 miles in all before I headed back to the house.

I walked into the house sweating and out of breath like I had just run from the police. When I got in the house Karen was sitting on the couch eating a bowl of cereal.

"Hey girl. Ya African King just left." She said poking fun.

"Who Kwazi?"

"Yeah girl who else? Ya'll get into a fight or something?"

"Why you ask me that?" I asked puzzled because I hadn't told her anything.

"Well when I told him you weren't here he aint believe me. Nigga checked your room and everything, then he left."

"Yeah we had a little fight. I'll explain it after I take a shower and change." I said.

"Okay girl I wanna hear all about it." Karen responded with her nosy ass.

I headed upstairs and into my room and immediately blew my top when I saw my pocketbook dumped out and all of my money gone. This no good piece of ish had taken my last. I let out a scream to the top of my lungs out of frustration. I couldn't believe he had done this to me. I had given Kwazi all of me, and he had promised to do the same. Even with everything I had been through in my life I had never felt a pain like this, and to top it all off Karen had already expected me to be moving so she told her sister she could have my room. I was totally screwed.

After doing some research I found out that Kwazi left me for another woman he had been seeing the entire time. I was blowing his phone up because the realtor had threatened to give the house to someone else if I didn't come up with the money ASAP. After calling and texting for days Kwazi finally answered.

"Waddup?" He answered as if I was bothering him.

"Kwazi I need that money or I'mma be homeless. Karen told her sister she could have my room because WE was supposed to be moving."

There was a long silence and a deep sigh before he responded.

"Aight look Lana. I'll give you your money back, but you gotta pay me back when you get your taxes in a few months."

I was flabbergasted.

"Yo are you fu…okay Kwazi I got you. Just please bring me the money before they give the crib to somebody else." I pleaded.

"Aight give me a few and I'll be over, but I aint playing I'm only loaning you this until you get your taxes." He reiterated.

"Okay Kwazi I got you. I put that on everything." I said as I hung up.

I could not believe this nigga was loaning me the money back that he had stolen from me. I mean the nerve of this cornball ass thief, but I had to agree to his terms in order to get the crib. As promised Kwazi came through and brought me the money.

"I'm serious Lana I want this back. We don't need to make this a problem." He said as he turned and left.

I slammed the door behind him, and went to get my new crib.

CHAPTER 13

After moving into the new place surprisingly enough Kwazi wouldn't leave me alone. Now it was him that was blowing up my phone. He admitted that he was with another woman but claimed that he still loved me and couldn't get me off of his mind. Truth be told I still loved him too, so I entertained his advances accepted my demotion as his side chick, I mean after all he was mine first.

It was so weird having Kwazi in my bed knowing that it would only be for an hour or so before he had to go home to his woman, who took him from me. The crazy part is I didn't even care as long as I could lease him for a few hours. I know; it was sad but true.

After a few months of being the side chick Kwazi and the home wrecker had broken up. The truth is she put him out after finding out that he was still seeing me.

"Look I know what I did to you was wrong, and I apologize. I mean I am really sorry for everything." Kwazi said with tears in his eyes as we lie in bed.

"I love you Kwazi but I can't trust you after what you did to me." I said being as honest as my heart would let me.

"Baby you got every right to feel the way you do, but I can show you better than I can tell you. Actions speak louder than words remember?"

The fact that I had never seen him cry had won me over.

"Okay Kwazi. I'mma give this a shot, but I swear if you hurt me again I…"

Kwazi shut me up with the most passionate kiss he had ever given me. And just like that we were together again.

****
****

The next 3 months went by flawlessly. Kwaz had converted back to the man I had once fell in love with. He was kind, caring, considerate, honest and most of all loyal. When I say I had no complaints; I aint even exaggerating. We had gone from being doomed to the couple of the year in just a few short months and I loved every second of it.

We were enjoying dinner one day when Kwazi grabbed my hand.

"Baby I want to let you know that I am so happy you took me back after everything that I had put you through." He said with the utmost sincerity in his eyes.

"Aww King that's the past, let's focus on the future." I said rubbing his hand with my thumb.

"Well we talked about the past and the future, but what about the present? You know what? Speaking of the present I got one for you."

With that being said Kwazi got up from the table and swung around to my side, where he got down on one knee and pulled a ring from his pocket. The faucet in my eyes immediately turned on full blast.

"Lana would you do me the honor of being my wife forever?" He said as his eyes welled up with tears.

"Baby you don't even have to ask." I responded as we both burst out into tears and held each other close.

A month later we were married at City Hall.

CHAPTER 14

A week after we were married Kwazi and I held hands as we walked through the grocery store. While walking through the isle I ran into Tye one of my old blood affiliates from my aunt's complex.

"Wassup Lana? Long time no see. How have you been? He said.

"I been good. Just got married. Tye this is my husband Kwazi, Kwazi this is my homeboy Tye."

"Hey wassup man? You used to own the chicken spot right?" Tye said extending his hand.

"Yeah that was my spot, and then wifey started taking all my time. You know how that goes." Kwazi laughed while dapping Tye up.

"Yeah no doubt. Well I'm happy for both of ya'll. Look I gotta go but I'mma tell Queenie and them I seen you. Come check us sometime." Tye said.

"Aight I just might do that." I responded.

"Take it easy bruh and congrats to both of ya'll." Tye said as he went on about his business.

Kwazi and I finished our shopping and then got in the car. I started the car and was about to put the car in gear when Kwazi hauled offed and backhanded me. I was dazed and saw starts and spots from the wicked hard blow.

"What? What was that for?" I said still in shock because I had never been hit by a man before let alone my gentle giant of a husband.

"Hoe if you ever disrespect me again and I'll kill you." Kwazi said through clenched teeth. His fist was now closed and balled up, but I knew who I was, so I still tried to explain myself.

"What are you talking about Kwazi? I never meant any disrespect, all we said to each other was …."

"Wamp!" Kwazi hit me so hard my head hit the driver side window.

"Hoe, did you hear what I said? I will tie you up, kill you, and hide your body… it better not happen again. Now drive."

That was the first time Kwazi had hit me, but it sure wasn't the last. I had suddenly become his punching bag almost on a daily basis. Kwazi had become extra violent and most times without provocation. He would punch me, kick me, drag me through the house by my hair, and send me to work battered and bruised at least 3 times a week. I cried out to his family, but they did nothing.

In months to come things with me and Kwazi hadn't changed much. He was still violent as hell and I was still too scared to leave. I had pretty much just accepted my life for what is was. One thing that changed was Kwazi started bring his family around more.

Kwazi's cousin Tracy started spending more and more time over at the house with us. Tracy and Kwazi were more like sister and brother. Their mothers were sisters and hated each other but Tracy and Kwazi were inseparable. I gotta admit I liked when Tracy came over, her and I were getting really cool with each other and Kwazi was always on his best behavior when she was around.

Tracy and I started doing girly things like shopping and mani/pedi dates. When I felt like we were close enough I told her about the abuse I had suffered at the hands of her cousin.

"Girl aint no man worth getting your brains beat in. You need to just leave my cousin if he doing all of that to you. I mean I love him to death but I don't play that woman beating shit. You need to let me check his ass for you."

"No Tracy please don't say anything. If you do I'mma have to pay the price when you aint around."

"Okay I aint gonna say nothing. But since he doesn't try that mess with me around, I'mma start staying over more."

"Thanks girl I appreciate it."

"No doubt. Now let's go get something to eat."

CHAPTER 15

As time went on I started hearing some weird things through the grapevine. I started hearing that Kwazi and Tracy were sleeping with each other. At first I defended them to no end. I'm telling everybody they are cousins and they are just really close. I also told them that Tracy was now like a sister to me as well. I refused to believe the storied, but then they were coming from different people who didn't even know each other. I'm hearing that they were in the club and dancing very provocative with one another, but hey that was subjective. Everybody has their own definition of provocative. So I let that go in one ear and out the other.

I was lying in bed one night while Kwaz was in the shower. His phone was lying on the nightstand and curiosity got the best of me. I grabbed it, cracked his password which was my birthday and read the first text message I saw.

Tracy: What you doing tomorrow?"

Kwazi: I'm doing you cuz as soon as Lana leave for work.

Tracy: No doubt. Love you cuz.

The rumors were true. I was furious, but I held my composure and pretended not to see a thing. The next morning, I got up and left the house for work like normal. Only I never left the block. I parked at the corner and waited patiently. Within the hour Tracy pulled up to the house and Kwazi let her in. I tried to brush if off as maybe I was losing my mind, or maybe misinterpreted the text. Even if it was true, do I have the nerve to walk in there and let Kwazi beat me to death. I pushed the thoughts to the back of mind, saying to myself "there just close" as I pulled off and just went to work.

That same night I was working late and I received a phone call from his friend Brian.

"Lana, did you know Kwazi and Tracy sleeping together" Brian said in shock and horror

"What are you talking about Brian, they are cousins? I replied in all dumbness.

"Lana, I went over to your house because I was supposed to be chilling with Brian. He gave me the spare key yesterday because he said he would be working out in the basement and probably wouldn't hear the bell" Brian continued

"Okay and…." I said getting irritated and having to get back to work.

"Well he wasn't answering his phone, so I figured he forgot, but when I drove by your house, I saw your car out front, so I used the key and went it." Brian took a breath and then continued…

"Well I heard moaning and thought Brian was just watching porn or something" Brian said laughing but I wasn't.

"I followed the moans all the way up to the bedroom where I opened the door and there he was. There was Kwazi with Tracy butt naked in the missionary position on my bed. I just stood there in shock and they jumped up in pure laughter. Kwazi was talking about he thought I was you, but felt better that is was only me. When Tracy tried to get up, Kwazi told her to lay back down. I slapped the shit out of him. Before I knew it they both turned on me and were beating on me. When it was over Tracy grabbed her clothes and left and I ran out to my car, pulled off and called you" Brian said all out of breath.

I hung up on Brian and immediately called Kwazi.

"Yo" Kwazi answered nonchalantly

"Yo, you sleeping with your cousin?" I gassed up the nerve to ask, knowing what he will do later.

"Who told you that, what are you talking about" He said not denying it like an innocent man would have.

"It don't matter you nasty son of a.." was all I can get out before he hung up on me and powered off his phone. I was heated. I went back to work and did what I needed to get out of there.

CHAPTER 16

Hours later, I was waiting on Kwazi to come and pick me up. He was running super late and not answering his phone. My blood boiled at the disrespect but I dare not say anything whenever he did show up.

About two hours later his cousin pulled up; now I was super pissed.

"Where the hell is my husband and where the hell is my car Kenny?" I screamed.

"Man I don't know where he at. He just hit me and asked me to come get you and take you home."

"This is some straight B.S. Kwazi always on one and being extra."

"Look I aint tryna get involved. I'm just doing what cuz asked me to do."

"Whatever Kenny. Just take me home." I snapped

Kenny did as he was told. When we got to my house my car wasn't there which meant Kwazi wasn't there. My house keys were on the car key ring so now I was locked out. With Kwazi ass still not answering his phone I called Karen and asked if I could crash at her house. She said yes and I had Kenny drop me off over there.

I couldn't sleep through the night wondering what the hell Kwazi was doing and why he wasn't returning my calls so as soon as daylight broke I asked Karen to take me home. When we pulled up I still didn't see my car, but decided to at least try and knock on the door. As I approached the door I was suddenly bum-rushed by a bunch of cops that seemed to come out of nowhere. It seemed like the whole precinct was there, maybe it was because the precinct was only a few blocks away. They threw me to the ground.

"Put your hands behind your back." The lead officer said.

"For what? I aint do nothing." I said kicking and fighting back.

"Just shut up and do as your told." He said cuffing me and leading me to the curb where there seemed to be a million cop cars pulling up and screeching to a halt.

As I got closer I could look inside all of the cop cars that were close to me and I could see my picture plastered all over there dashboards and on board computers.

"WTF is going on?" I asked, but was ignored as I was violently pushed into the backseat of a squad car.

I was nervous and trembling as I asked again.

"Officer please tell me what's going on." I pleaded

They stayed silent all the way to the precinct. When we got there they took me straight into the interrogation room.

"Look Lana we found a body."

"Oh my God my husband is dead?" I screamed as I started to cry hysterically.

"Of course he is and you killed him." The officer said sarcastically.

"What? No? I would never do anything to hurt him."

"Then you tell me what Brian did to deserve being murdered in cold blood."

"What... Brian?" I asked now really confused as to what was going on.

"That's ya husband aint it?"

"No. My husband's name is Kwazi."

"Yeah well Brian was found dead in your car. Now you wanna come clean and tell us what happened?"

"Listen I was at work all night last night. There is no way I could have done any of this, Brian is a friend of my husband."

"You was at work huh?"

"Yeah call my boss. Check the video tapes." I yelled

Those bastards kept me there for 22 hours grilling me over and over again, but my answers never changed and I never wavered because I truly had no idea what was going on. As it turned out they knew I was innocent because they found Kwazi's wallet next to the body, and they had checked my alibi 21 hours ago, they just tried to break me for information that I didn't even have.

After seeing that I was a lost cause they let me go. A few hours later they tracked Kwazi down and brought him in for questioning. Kwazi claims that

Brian was his friend, and asked for a ride to go meet somebody in the park about some money. Kwaz said the guy he took Brian to meet was pressing Brian about some money that was owed. Kwaz said Brian instructed the guy to get in, and told me to pull off so I did. He went on to say that when they stopped the car the guy they met up with then tried to rob him. He said the strange guy pulled out a knife, he gave him his wallet and got out and ran. He said that he ran leaving Brian with the guy. They had no other evidence to hold Kwaz so they let him go. Kwazi was only in the precinct for three hours.

"Well damn Kwaz how you get out so fast?" I asked.

"Cuz I kept my mouth shut and just told then what happened. Point blank. We gonna need a new car."

"Damn Kwaz this is the 5th car you done cost me. You crashed four and now this one is impounded as part of a murder scene."

"Look I was just questioned for a murder I didn't do. You think I give a fuck about your funky ass car?

I could see his temper flaring so I just let it go. The most important thing was we were home, free, and safe. By the graces of God, we had dodged a bullet with Brian's murder. They had nothing on Kwaz and they damn sure aint have nothing on me so it was a dead issue; no pun intended. Deep down inside, I feel I know what really happened to Brian....

CHAPTER 17

The prayers didn't stop the beatings, but my inner peace and my new relationship with God numbed the pain. In between beatings I found myself on the internet doing research and learning the whole social media thing. That's where I met James. Well, I actually met James at work, but with my abusive husband constantly popping up, I was only able to talk to James on social media. James was sweet, he transferred from our location to an out of state location causing him to move, what felt like a billion miles away. However, he always seemed to be right there when I needed a friend. James knew about Kwazi and everything that I was going through. I know it sounds crazy but a complete stranger was my only friend. James would emotionally console me when Kwazi physically abusing me. He also booked me a hotel one when Kwazi would beat me and then leave, and I would be scared of his return. And then one day I got the sign. In routine conversation I told James the name of the company I wanted to soon work, for and he told me they had an office in his town. I told him I knew what I needed to do, and although I appreciated him, I was stuck in between survival and abuse. In true gentleman fashion James told me he understood. He stated, I have to make up in my and what I wanted to do. He said whatever I choose, I need to know that it's what I want and no one else.

The day of my 21st birthday I sat in the house depressed because it was my milestone birthday, the day that I had legally become a woman and my husband didn't even acknowledge my special day. Meanwhile James had been trying to make me smile all day via text and Facebook.

"Why in the hell you just sitting there looking all stupid?" Kwazi said noticing my foul mood.

"Maybe it's because my birthday is almost over and my sorry ass husband aint even acknowledge it."

"Oh you want me to acknowledge your birthday? Okay let's go let me show everybody how much I love my birthday on her special day."

Kwazi grabbed me by my hair and started punching me in the face splitting my skin open with every punch. He then dragged me outside and down the street while I was kicking and screaming for help; help that came from no one. Everyone just stood by and watched as Kwazi administered the worst beating he had given me since I had known him.

"Let's go. Take them damn clothes off. It's ya birthday so you should be in ya birthday suit." He said ripping my clothes off in the middle of the street.

"Kwazi please stop." I cried out, but my cries fell on deaf ears as he continued his rampage.

"Nah you 21 so I'mma whoop that ass for 21 minutes. You wanted attention on your special day so I'm giving it to you."

This sick bastard kept looking at his watch and when the 21st minute mark hit he stopped in full swing and left me naked, bleeding, and beaten half to death in the middle of the street two blocks away.

I literally crawled back to the house and passed out on the living room floor. When I woke up there was a Facebook message from James.

"So is the birthday girl gonna let me see that beautiful face on her special day?"

I took my camera phone and sent James a selfie so he could see how my birthday turned out. Happy Birthday to me…yeah right.

CHAPTER 18

After what happened on my birthday James immediately paid for a plane ticket for me to come to South Carolina. He said he wouldn't take no for an answer so the next day I pretended to go to work with both eyes swollen and all and headed straight to Newark International Airport. When I go to Delta I pulled up and left my car right there.

"Ma'am you can't park there." A cop yelled.

"Tow it." I yelled back as I kept it moving for the ticket counter.

The looks people gave me as I made my way through the terminal made me feel like I was some type of animal that escaped from the zoo. This was my first time on a plane, but I was too anxious to be afraid as the large, winged, hunk of metal took off down the runway and into the sky. When we got high enough for me to look out the window and see the clouds I finally felt at peace.

James had promised to take care of me and love me the way I deserved to be loved. And although I had heard that from every man I had ever encountered, once again I believed that this man would be different, but this time I prayed on it.

James had told me that I could stay with him until I was healed enough to start the new job, save up and get my own place which he would help me do without hesitation. I had told my job that I had to leave town indefinitely do to an emergency and I asked for an emergency lateral transfer. I'm sure they knew I was running away from Kwazi; I mean they had seen the results of his love time and time again so they granted the transfer with no questions asked and wished me the best.

I asked James if he wouldn't mind getting me a new cell phone since I wanted no ties to Kwazi and definitely didn't want him tracking me. Of course he obliged. James was everything that every other man in my life wasn't, but what drew me to him more than anything was the fact that he was into church and not into the streets.

James and I attended church regularly. He introduced me to the Pastor and the congregation who all welcomed me with opened arms. I connected with a few of the in the church, and became a part of the youth ministry as well a mime leader. I got a few stare downs when people realized I was with James, because of the age difference, and regardless of his age, he was definitely a catch. It wasn't long before James and I got serious. A month after I arrived I was pregnant with James' child. When I found out I was with child I dropped to my knees and thanked God that I lived long enough to even bring another life into the world. Times when I thought death would take me out, God gave me life. I had been through hell in my short lived 21 years on this earth, and it wasn't until I put my faith in God that his light started to shine down on me.

God had given me everything I ever needed; at 24, I had a new life, a career at one of the most prestigious hospital systems, a loving man, a great church family and an intelligent, loving and caring son. I had never been happier and at peace than I was at that very moment in my life. So that's how it ends; with a new beginning.

You see for all of the years that I endured the mental, physical, and psychological abuse and torment; I had never truly given myself to God. Like many; it took for me to hit rock bottom to ask God to save me and just like the merciful God that he is he waved his hands over me and draped me in his heavenly glory and light. I realized all those times I prayed, it wasn't God that wasn't hearing me, it was me that wasn't hearing him. His first commandment is "Thou shall not have any other God's before me". When I converted Muslim, I denounced who God was. Though he could have let me die in my struggle, he still claimed me as a child of God. Although I turned my back on him, he never turned his back on me. See, "the race is not given to the swift, but to those who can endure to the end" and, "All things work together for good, for those who love God and are called according to his purpose". He knew what I was predestined to be, before I entered this world. He knew I would be strong enough to survive the battles and show the world what God was able to do, and thats exceedingly above all we can ask. My trials have caused pain, but my triumph has been better.

I am happy to say that James and I are still together. We have a beautiful son and a beautiful life together. I am now a very active member of the church as well as a public speaker. I minister to young ladies who are going through the same things I went through. I tell them that giving up is easy, killing yourself is easy, but having faith is what we shoot for.

The diploma I received from the night school was a joke. I came to find out the school wasn't accredited. When I got to South Carolina, I got my GED, Diploma in Medical Office Management, and Degree in Healthcare Management.

Faith of a mustard seed is all the good book says we need.

I am a living testimony, that if you call on God, and show him that you are ready to devote your life to Christ, he will come and he will work miracles on your life you never imagined could happen. He will save you. He will be there through the good and the bad, directing your transformation from Victim to Victorious. Take it from me; God gets your messages he just wants you to call more often.

GOD BLESS YOU ALL,

CHAINAH

Made in the USA
Columbia, SC
01 March 2020